# Winter Trials
# By K.S. Marsden

To

Beth

Happy Reading

K.S. M

Printed by CreateSpace, an Amazon.com Company

ISBN-13: 978-1534803589

ISBN-10: 1534803580

Winter Trials was originally published in "Echoes of Winter", a compilation of short stories by a group of YA authors.

They share a little bit of magic, romance, and festive feelings!

This ebook can be downloaded for free from most online retailers.

Check out my website for more useful links:

kellymarsden.wix.com/home

**Chapter One**

Mid-December brought with it a new flurry of snow, cementing the fact that it was well and truly winter. It might make the rolling Yorkshire countryside pleasant and picturesque when the sun finally got out, but right now it was a harsh grey world, driven on a cold wind.

Mark pulled his collar up against his scarf, and made sure his hat was secure. It may only be a short run from the bus to the school buildings, but it was sure to be bloody cold. Outside, he slipped and skidded on the snow compacted to ice by his fellow students, and was glad to get into the main school building.

Out of habit, he nodded to the other Year 11 students he was friends with, but he kept a sharp eye out for his best friend. Harry was standing further down the corridor, looking half-hypnotised and half-annoyed.

"What's up with you?" Mark asked.

"I've just come from orchestra practise. Because of some annoying Year 7 brats pestering Mr Smith, he agreed to 'let' us play Christmas carols for the whole bloody session." Harry shook his head. "It's like I can still hear Rudolph, I can't get rid of it."

Mark grinned at his friend's discomfort as he led the way to class. Luckily his school had put hooks at the back of each classroom for their coats – it made it feel like they were back in primary school, but at least their cold, wet coats would dry over the hot radiators.

"Do you know how boring it is to play Rudolph?" Harry continued, not finished with his rant. "I mean sure, if it's just guitars, we get all sorts of chords, layers and stuff. But *this*… in the lesser part of the orchestra, we get one note every bar or so. Dun… dun… d-"

"OK, I get it." Mark cut in, aware of all the weird looks they were receiving from the rest of the class. He sat down and hurried to pull Harry into the seat next to him.

"I'm just saying, it's a completely classist issue. String snobs come first – of which we're exiled. Then the wind; then brass; and then us lowly guitar players."

"And I've told you before, if it's such a big deal – quit. Or start holding your guitar like a cello." Mark retorted, somewhat tired of this argument from Harry. Maybe he should've let him carry on with the Christmas carol rant.

Harry's attention was fortunately stolen by Mrs Green, as their History teacher tried to get them to remember what had been covered just yesterday.

An hour later and the bell rang. Mark grabbed his stuff and made his way to his next class.

"So, Mark, can you help me with Christmas shopping this weekend?" Harry asked as soon as they were out of Mrs Green's control.

Mark looked to Harry, why didn't it surprise him that he still had gifts to get the very weekend before Christmas. "Sure."

"Good, I need your help to find something for Sarah."

Mark rolled his eyes. Sarah was a lovely girl, and Mark hoped that Harry could go a whole term without screwing up their relationship. "Why d'you need me?"

"She won't tell me what she wants, only does that annoying girl-thing and just hints." Harry grinned. "Besides, Sarah *talks* to you."

"She talks to me as much as any other guy." Mark retorted. "I just listen instead of thinking about her boobs."

"So do you think we can get something in Tealford?" Harry asked, glossing over his friend's comment.

"Er, no. Try the Fashion Outlet near York?" Mark replied, as he hovered by the Chemistry classroom. "Unless you want to jump on the train and risk Meadowhell?"

Mark chuckled at his friend's look of horror.

"So who will you be kissing under the mistletoe?" Harry asked, changing the subject to Mark's own weakness.

Mark grit his teeth and gave a forced smile. "Nobody."

"There's always Dean." Harry goaded.

Mark thumped him on the arm, then pulled his books out before the teacher had a go at them. "One of these days, I'm gonna deck ya."

Mark hunkered down as his teacher started the day's lecture. As they were the only openly gay students at Tealford High School, people seemed to expect Mark and Dean to get together. Unfortunately, Mark couldn't stand Dean; and he didn't care to find out how the other felt about him. Which didn't stop Harry from using it as a very lowly attack.

*****

When the dinner bell went, Sarah came bounding up. She gave Harry a sweet kiss, and a smiling hello to Mark.

"Have you guys decided if you're going to the Christmas do yet?" She asked, looking between them. The posters had only been up a few hours, but as far as Sarah was concerned, decisions shouldn't take half that long.

Mark sighed, Friday the 21st wasn't only the school party, it was the Winter Solstice. "I dunno, I might have a family thing on."

Sarah's eyes widened. "Oh yeah, isn't it time for your grandmother's voodoo stuff?"

Mark stared at her, completely off balance from her comment. He glanced at Harry and noticed his best friend stifling his laughter. "What misinformation have you been feeding her?"

"C-couldn't… resist…" Harry choked.

"Sarah, do me a favour... don't believe a word this arse tells you about my family." Mark said, leading the way to the trays of hot pizza and chips.

"So it's not true that your grandmother is a witch?" Sarah asked, nudging him out of the way so she could get a plate. "Everyone in Tealford knows that."

Mark glanced up at the dinner lady, but the middle aged woman was paying no attention to the teenagers. "Sure, Nanna's a witch, but none of that 'voodoo stuff'."

Mark paid and walked to an empty table, waiting for the other two to join him. Harry sat down and immediately got stuck into his dinner. Sarah was a little more distracted, finding something of interest in the far corner.

"That must be the new guy Stephanie was on about." She said conspiratorially, ducking down before she was caught staring. "He's cute."

Harry's head snapped up, his cheeks full of pizza and a smear of tomato sauce on his lips.

"Tsk. Not as cute as you, of course, Harry." She said, almost sincere.

Mark twisted in his chair, trying to see what the fuss was about. He couldn't see much through the crowded hall, a mere glimpse of dark blond hair. "What's his story?"

New pupils were rare at Tealford High School. When they were eleven years old, the kids from all of the surrounding villages and hamlets made the daily trek to Tealford. Five years later, they graduated. Nobody young ever moved to this area. Sure, a few retirees came this way after a lifetime in the city, dreaming of 'The Good Life', but never anyone their age. Mark supposed that was enough to spark the school's interest. It also didn't hurt if he was cute.

"He's from London," Sarah replied, "I heard that his parents died recently and he's moved Up North to live with his aunt."

"A Londoner?" Harry asked, craning his neck to see the alien.

"A Londoner? Maybe he'll be a bit more open-minded than these country boys."

The trio looked up to see Dean hovering by their table.

"I don't remember asking you." Mark retorted.

Dean ignored him, gazing across at the new guy. "I love his hair, it's got to be a dye job though – nobody has dark gold hair like that. Ugh, couldn't you just imagine running your hands-"

"Dean!" Sarah was the first to snap. "Seriously, not every thought you have is golden, enough with the sharing."

Dean huffed and carried his tray away, finding a table of girls that were giggling over the new arrival.

Harry paused with a forkful of chips halfway to his mouth. "He does have a point…"

"You did not just say that?" Mark asked, as he joined Sarah in laughter.

"No, shut up, not the running your hands through his hair thing!" Harry argued, blushing bright red. "I mean, he could be, y'know, gay."

Mark rolled his eyes. "Any guy in the world could be gay, Harry. It doesn't take a London accent and trendy highlights."

Mark chuckled as Harry threw a burnt chip at his head, in retaliation.

As they got a warning look from the supervising teacher, Mark quickly changed the subject.

"I was gonna ask you guys if you wanted to come to mine for the Winter Solstice. We usually have a party every year, and Nanna's been nagging me about not bringing any friends." Mark asked, not meeting their eyes. "I mean, I'll understand if you'd rather go to the school party."

"Yes!" Sarah piped up, excited at the prospect of getting an inside look at a witch's Winter Solstice. "I mean, yeah, that sounds fun."

Harry looked a little more dubious. "We won't have to dance naked around a fire, or anything?"

"No, that's only optional." Mark answered with a shake of his head. Nudity and the Yorkshire winter didn't go together well. "There is a bonfire, but it's basically just an opportunity to eat, drink and be merry. There's very little witchy stuff that goes on."

Mark gathered his coat and bag and headed towards the common room, which was sure to be packed on a wet, miserable day like today.

"Hey, maybe you could invite the new guy to your party." Sarah suggested.

Mark rolled his eyes. "Sure, I'll just ask the good-looking stranger if he wants to come round to my Nanna's and dance naked around a fire."

Mark was suddenly aware of the engulfing silence.

"Who'll be naked doing what now?"

Mark turned at the oddly-accented voice, to face the last person he expected to see. The new guy gazed curiously at him, his blue eyes sparkling with amusement. He stood as tall as Mark, and close up he was just as handsome as everyone had said.

"I-I, um…" Mark tried to gulp down his nerves, but the embarrassment just crept back up.

Thankfully Sarah jumped in to rescue him. "Hey, you're the new guy! How are you enjoying Tealford?"

He looked down at Sarah with a wary smile. "Good thanks, and I think I should change my name to 'New Guy'."

Sarah rocked onto the balls of her feet, excited by the direct contact of his electric blue eyes. She blushed as she replied, "What's your real name? I'm Sarah, this is Harry and Mark."

"Damian." He replied, glancing distractedly down the corridor. "I've gotta go, um… I might see you around."

Without waiting for a response, Damian traipsed off down the corridor, leaving the trio watching him disappear.

Sarah bounced on the balls of her feet, gripping Harry's arm. "Ugh, if I was single right now, I'd stalk that boy until he loved me."

"Psycho much?" Mark teased.

"Yeah, and luckily the guy you're with is pretty awesome, and didn't just hear that." Harry added drily.

"Aw, you know I love you most." Sarah replied, pouting.

Mark saw his cue to leave, as the two started to spout nonsense which would inevitably lead to kissing. Harry and Sarah might think they were the new Romeo and Juliet, but when they snogged in public, it was just plain gross.

## Chapter Two

As school ended, the snow had turned to sleet; wet and very cold on the biting wind.

Mark wrapped up and hovered in the relative shelter of the school wall. Harry and Sarah had already disappeared on their bus that circled the villages to the south, leaving Mark to wait for the bus to travel the west route.

Out of the corner of his eye, Mark spotted a very fashionable trench coat, with a very blue face above it.

"Y'look bloody frozen." Mark ejected.

Damian gave him a withering look, his jaw clamped shut to stop his teeth chattering.

"Don't you have a warm coat?"

"This is…" Damian stuttered. "It did the job down south."

"Well, it won't do for a Yorkshire winter." Mark gestured at the sleet. "This is nowt yet. It gets worse."

Damian swore beneath his breath. He looked up as a car's headlights swung round in their direction.

"That's my aunt. See you tomorrow, Mark." For a moment his blue eyes met Mark's, then Damian hurried off to the waiting jeep, head tucked down.

Mark watched him leave for the second time that day. Well, the good news was he hadn't mentioned nudity, and he'd managed to address Damian in full sentences that even made sense. The bad news, he must have sounded like an old woman, wittering on about the weather.

The school bus finally crawled up, beeping its horn to announce its late arrival. Mark filed on with the rest of the impatient students.

The bumpy ride was a bit of a blur, and in no time Mark was clambering down from the bus, before starting the half-mile trek to his house. His parents wouldn't be home from work for another hour and a half. His Mum worked as a nurse in the local GP surgery, and his Dad... well his Dad did some sort of office job that Mark didn't entirely understand. At least Nanna was likely to be in her half of the house.

The big old farmhouse had originally been a single home, but before Mark had been born, his grandad had decided he was getting too old to maintain the big house. It was logical to split the place into two, giving the larger half to the young, newly-married couple that were Mark's Mum and Dad.

Since his grandad had passed away a couple of years ago, it seemed only right that Nanna got both her independence and privacy, plus her family close by.

Mark marched up the driveway, the melted snow sloshing underfoot. He caught some movement to his far right, and looked up to see Nanna walking slowly through the garden, a broom held above her head.

Mark sighed and headed towards her. "Nanna, you're not helping overcome the stereotypes when you do this stuff."

"Stay there." She warned, not taking her eyes off the old coal house. "That evil bloody tabby cat from Mr Hick's place has been harassing poor Tigger again."

The old woman stalked forward, fixated on her target. Suddenly she swing her brush down and started shouting like a banshee. There was a brown and orange streak across the grey ground.

"And stay out, you-"

Mark laughed as his Nanna broke into a swearing tirade after the disappearing cat.

"Hmph, I don't know what you're laughing at, young man. You'd do the same if you'd seen that mangy thing having a go at Tigger." She huffed again and turned back to the house, walking straight to the kitchen.

Despite the cold, the old woman was wearing nothing more than her old house cardigan. She always claimed that the cold didn't bother her, and that everyone else was just being nesh. Mark wondered if the immunity to cold was a witch thing.

He followed her into the warm kitchen, and drifted over to the Aga. Tigger was sprawled in front of it, his tail lazily flicking. Nanna had gotten him as a kitten, to help keep the mice away. Inspired by his orange coat and white paws, the young Mark had insisted calling him Tigger.

He never did chase mice much; Tigger had wrapped the family around his paw, and became a pampered house cat.

"Can't you do something witchy to keep the tabby away?" Mark asked.

Nanna snorted as she put hot water in the teapot, before putting the tea tray on the kitchen table. "No, for such a small thing, it wouldn't be worth the potential consequences."

Mark leant over and stole a biscuit to go with his cuppa.

"Have you asked Harry and his girlfriend to come to the Winter Solstice?" Nanna asked, as she had for the past fortnight.

"Ha, I actually have. They said yes." Mark replied.

Nanna raised a brow in surprise at her grandson's confidence.

"Why are you so keen for them to come this year?"

Nanna sipped her tea, taking her time. "You're sixteen now."

"Yeah, I'd noticed." Mark remarked, sneaking a second biscuit. Mark hadn't made a huge deal when he turned sixteen at the end of November, he'd just gone ice-skating with a group of friends. But his parents had been uncharacteristically serious, giving him a lecture on how to be a grown-up. Oh, and they didn't hesitate in hinting that he could get a job now.

Nanna frowned at his sarcasm. "The truth is, Mark, you come from a long line of witches."

"I know," Mark shrugged, "you've always been very open about the family history."

"What do you think about learning actual witchcraft?"

Mark looked up at her with surprise. "Me?"

"No, Harry." Nanna retorted. "Yes, you, you silly boy."

"I don't know, I've never thought about it." Mark answered truthfully. He'd grown up knowing about witches, and witnessing the parties and proceedings throughout the year. It all seemed a normal part of his life and he'd never questioned it.

"Well, I promised to wait until you were sixteen, before I brought it up. Your parents wanted you to concentrate on school and have a relatively normal childhood. Now you're old enough to make your own decisions, whether that is to learn witchcraft; or going on as you were before." Nanna cradled her cup.

"I turned sixteen a couple of weeks ago, why the delay?"

"I've been waiting for you to finally work up the nerve and ask your friends to the winter festivities." Nanna replied, threatening him with a teaspoon. "I think it's important that Harry is involved. You two have been best friends forever – I want you to feel that you can talk to him about it."

Mark frowned. "Nanna, it's a decision about whether or not I want to take up witchcraft – I'm not moving to a monastery, lighten up!"

Nanna pursed her thin lips.

"Why did Dad decide not to do it?" Mark asked.

"It was his choice, you'll have to ask him." Nanna replied. She had never tried to force her son to join her way of life, but she had to admit that she was looking forward to potentially teaching somebody.

She got up and moved over to the doorway – on a shelf above it were a collection of small hardback books. Nanna ran her hand over the spines before finally selecting one. "Here, a taster for you. There shouldn't be any consequences to practising this."

Mark took the offered book gingerly. He was half-expecting fireworks, shivers up his spine, or something witchy. Nothing.

The little book had a faded dark-red cover, and when he flicked it open, he saw a fine-printed page, its margins covered in annotations.

"Auras?" He asked, glancing at the title.

"Aye, you can take it as extra homework. That book's taught a lot of people and, whether or not you take up witchcraft, it is invaluable to recognise the auras of those around you."

Mark sighed and put the book into his rucksack. "Speaking of homework, I've a massive essay to write. Thanks for the cuppa, Nanna."

## Chapter Three

Mark sat on the school bus as it ambled down the still-dark country lanes, the snow-laden stone walls bobbing at various heights past the window. It was supposed to be sunny this morning, or so the weatherman said. All that meant to Mark, was the cloudless night translated into lots of ice. Not his favourite.

Mark was taking advantage of the ride, reading the book on auras before he had to switch into school mode. It was pretty dense and dull stuff – only the personal comments scribbled in the borders made it more bearable than a school textbook. There were a lot of comments about clearing your mind, to increase your perception – not likely on a bus filled with school kids.

"Is this seat taken?"

Mark looked up at the speaker and was surprised to see Damian standing there.

"Yes - I mean, no." Mark pulled his rucksack off the spare seat. "Sit down."

Mark glanced about the bus, there were a few spare seats next to other students, but Damian had decided to sit next to him! His internal cartwheels collapsed when he realised that he might be the only student Damian knew at the moment.

"I thought your aunt drove you to school?" Mark asked.

"She only made the effort for my first day. I think she wanted to make sure I actually attended school." Damian glanced down at the book in Mark's lap. "Reading anything good?"

"No… um, sort of. It's just a book my Nanna gave me."

"The same Nanna that has you all dancing naked round a fire?"

Mark felt a wave of heat prickling up his neck. "I was hoping you didn't hear all that."

"I heard enough." Damian replied, smirking. "It was actually the most entertaining thing I heard all day."

"Don't worry, it's just a joke. Built on the misconceptions of the many." Mark answered, before realising how much of an idiot he sounded. He bit the inside of his lip and looked out at the scene of glittering fields.

"Huh." Without a word, Damian plucked the little red hardback book out of his hands and flicked to the cover page. "Auras?"

"Hey, give it back!" Mark argued. "I thought Londoners were allergic to conversing with strangers on buses."

"Maybe I'm embracing Northern customs. Besides, you're not a stranger, we met yesterday. I even know your name." Damian shrugged, but didn't take his eyes off the writing. "So… auras?"

"It's nothing… it's… OK, if I'm honest, what I've read of it is kinda cool. It's about seeing past the image people project, and seeing the aura of their true selves. Maybe I could use you as my guinea pig – see whether you're north or south!"

Damian smiled, although this time it didn't reach his cool blue eyes. He closed the book and handed it back to Mark. "I don't think I'd make a very interesting subject."

The bus jerked as the brakes went on and everyone began to move, ready to file off. Were they at school already?

Mark pulled his coat on and when he turned back, Damian had already gone. He swore silently and berated himself. He'd sounded like a freak, maybe he should stick to talking about the weather next time. If there was a next time; Damian was probably not going to make the mistake of sitting next to him again.

Mark made his way off the bus, thinking of nothing more than getting through this blasted day. As soon as he stepped onto the icy pavement, his feet slipped from under him. Mark yelped as his backside hit the hard ground. He was aware of the laughter of others around him. This was definitely one of the worst starts to the day he'd had in a while.

A gloved hand was offered, and Mark took it thankfully. Less than gracefully, he got to his feet. Mark froze when he saw his helper.

"You?"

"I could have just pointed and laughed like the others." Damian replied, shrinking away. "Sorry if I seem to be stalking you – I'm not, by the way. I just… I don't know many people yet and-"

"No! That's… sorry I was being rude." Mark interrupted. It was odd to witness babbling from someone else. He found it strangely endearing from Damian; although Mark imagined his own babbling was considered annoying. "I only thought that with me being weird on the bus, you would've scarpered."

"You weren't weird." Damian responded, then amended his statement, "OK, you weren't *that* weird."

Mark gave a crooked smile and started to walk towards school.

"So what's it all about?" Damian asked. "The aura and the ritual stuff?"

Mark glanced over his shoulder, but saw nobody near; although it was hardly a secret. "My Nanna's a witch."

"Seriously?"

"Yeah, I'm afraid so."

"And what about you?" Damian asked.

"What do you mean?"

"Are you a witch, too?" He shrugged. "You *were* reading a book about auras on the school bus."

"I guess I'm a witch-in-training." Mark replied hesitantly. "It turns out Nanna was waiting until I was sixteen to see if I wanted to learn about witchcraft."

"And do you? Want to be a witch and everything?"

"I dunno, I guess so. I mean, I won't have to do anything I don't want to do, and a bit more knowledge can't hurt." Mark looked over at Damian. "Sorry, I don't know why I'm telling you all this."

"S'alright. It's good to have someone to talk to." Damian replied. "My aunt tiptoes around me at home, afraid I'm going to break if she says the wrong thing. So she tends to say nothing at all."

"Yeah." Mark replied, feeling awkward broaching such a terrible topic. "I heard about your parents, I'm sorry."

Damian sighed. "Everyone's so sorry. Can we not talk about it?"

"Sure." Mark replied quickly. He felt relieved that Damian had closed the topic, then immediately felt guilty for it.

He looked up and saw Harry and Sarah waiting for him outside History class. They both looked surprised at the company Mark kept.

"Hi Damian." Sarah greeted. "Are you in History with us?"

"Hi... Sarah, isn't it?" Damian looked down at the bubbly girl. "No, I'm taking Geography GCSE instead."

"That's down the corridor, last door on the left." Harry said, gesturing that way.

"OK, guess I'll see you all later."

"Yeah, you should join us at dinner." Mark said, wanting to take advantage of being on friendly terms. "I mean, if you don't have any other plans.

"That sounds cool." The bell rang and Damian gave an awkward half-wave, and made his way to Geography.

Mark turned to see the questioning faces of his two friends, but he wasn't in any rush to give answers. "Shall we get to class?"

"Since when are you the swot?" Harry retorted, but filed into the History classroom.

## Chapter Four

That afternoon, as his RE teacher droned on, Mark's thoughts turned to the book Nanna had given him. To practise reading auras he needed a clear mind, and people to watch. Luckily, he had both at this point; Mark rarely paid attention in RE. His teacher, Mr Burns, seemed content with his students being present while he lectured on, participation was hardly necessary.

Mark was struck by the irony of wanting to practise witchcraft in the middle of Religious Education, but he wasn't hurting anyone.

He focussed on the girl in front of him, feeling a little frustrated that he couldn't see anything out of the ordinary. Mark sat back in his chair, mentally running through the instructions. That in itself seemed to steady his thoughts and move them away from his primary level of awareness. Taking a deep breath, he looked again.

Mark almost jolted out of his relaxed state as he realised that he could see a brown haze emanating from the girl. It was as substantial as fog, and seemed to drift and fade. The aura pulsed again into being, following the girl as she fidgeted in her seat.

Mark coughed to hide his victorious smile, then brought himself to his usual level of awareness. He glanced up at the front of the classroom, afraid his teacher would have noticed; but no, Mr Burns was still rattling on about the topic du jour.

Keen to see if he could do it again, Mark steadied his breathing and allowed his focus to shift. It came easier this time, and soon he could see the brown aura around 'Little-Miss-Fidget' in front of him.

Mark tried to keep his concentration steady, as he moved his focus to someone else. It was harder than he thought and he struggled to maintain the link. As his eyes fell on Harry, a blue aura blossomed, as his best friend focussed on Sarah. If Mark had to guess, Harry's thoughts were also firmly not on Religious Education. Mark was pretty sure blue was linked to, ah, affection.

Mark tried to keep his smile to himself, and he shifted his focus again. Curiously, he looked towards Damian, who finally shared a class with them. The poor guy was sat up front, in the only spare seat in Mr Burns' archaic seating plan.

A white aura shimmered up from his skin, so beautiful that it mesmerised Mark. It was almost a relief, that his initial opinion of Damian was correct. It would have been embarrassing if he'd been fooled by a pretty face. It was... Mark's breath caught as he saw a black stain on the edge of Damian's white aura. It grew, and swallowed all the light, then receded as though it had never been there.

Damian tensed in his seat on the front row, and annoyed, he looked behind him. Was it disappointment in his eyes when he saw Mark looking his way?

Mark felt his tenuous hold on his calm state break away and the aura vanished from the new guy. It was supposed to be to be harmless, viewing the auras of those around him. So why did Mark suddenly feel guilty? That he'd witnessed something he shouldn't have?

The last bell rang; Damian jumped up and was the first out of class.

Mark dejectedly grabbed his things and made his way outside. The bright and beautiful day had quickly become overcast; Mark sighed at the prospect of heavy snow. At least it would stop him slipping on the ice for a day or two.

He made his way carefully to the west villages' bus and clambered aboard without any major incident. He looked along the half-filled seats, and saw Damian sitting, his head against the cold window.

"This seat taken?" Mark asked nervously.

Damian shrugged; it wasn't exactly a resounding plea to join him, but Mark took it as the permission he needed.

The bus engine rumbled to life and it soon set off, carrying its noisy cargo away from Tealford High.

Mark racked his brain for something to say, but every thought dried and crumbled. He didn't need to perceive auras to see the wall that Damian had thrown up. Damian stared resolutely out of the window at the grey passing scene.

The silence between them dragged on, as the rest of the bus continued to swell with the daily gossip that held the excited edge that came with heading home.

Eventually Damian looked up at Mark. "Can I get by?" He asked dully.

Mark felt a pang of disappointment as he got out of the way so Damian could get out of the window seat. Mark wasn't the only person watching Damian leave the bus; most of the girls were distracted by the hot new guy walking past.

*****

The snow started to fall as Mark walked home from the bus stop. It was delicate and deceptively light, but he knew it wouldn't be long before the real snow.

Mark went straight into his Nanna's house, unable to shake his thoughts of today.

"Ah, it's yourself." She greeted as he walked into her warm kitchen. Nanna moved to put the kettle onto the Aga.

While she was putting together the tea tray, Mark hung up his wet coat and sat by the kitchen table. A large orange fur ball jumped onto his lap, and immediately started purring. Mark scratched Tigger's favourite spot under his chin, then stroked his thick winter coat; the cat's purrs vibrating through his hand.

Nanna took one look at the cat on his lap and frowned. "What's wrong?"

"How did you-?"

"Tigger only acts like that when you're upset; or I'm taking him to the vets." Nanna replied, setting the tea things on the table. "Spill."

"Traitor." Mark said, poking Tigger's well-covered ribs. The cat looked up innocently, then curled up on his lap. "It's nothing… it's… I tried the aura reading."

Mark broke off and pulled the little red book from his bag.

"Oh? How did it go?" Nanna asked, looking very pleased at this big step.

"Well, it wasn't easy," Mark remarked, grabbing a biscuit, "but I did it. It was oddly relaxing. I saw Harry's – his was blue."

"Which pertains to love." Nanna added.

Mark nodded. "Yeah, he was looking at Sarah at the time, so that's what I thought. Does that mean he loves her?"

Mark already knew the answer, but he felt a little hurt. He was jealous – not that he had ever had those type of feelings for Harry; but rather that his best friend was being stolen away by something so consuming. He did his best to ignore how lonely it was to be a gay teenager.

"I would imagine he does," Nanna answered, "it's always love and passion at sixteen "

Mark groaned. "OK, well there was another girl who had this brown aura."

Nanna frowned. "That usually means they are conflicted."

Mark nodded. "Yeah, that's what the book said; and it fits, Michelle is usually causing trouble."

Nanna tapped her mug of tea as she stared at her grandson. "People are rarely bad for the sake of it. There's usually something it stems from."

Mark thought back to Michelle, she was always fidgety and had more than her share of teenage angst. "The result is the same, she's not a nice person."

"I want you to talk to her."

"What? But I-"

Nanna held up a hand to silence him. "You have seen her aura, you have witnessed that something is distressing her. It is your duty to act on it. It may be that she will reject your friendship, but how would you feel if you did nothing and she did something extreme as a result of her problems?"

Mark groaned and dropped his head on the table. "Fine, I'll speak to her tomorrow." Came the muffled reply.

Mark sat up again, aware that his school jumper was now covered in orange cat hair.

"There was a third guinea pig." He said slowly, wanting to phrase it right. "This new guy, Damian. He had a white aura.

"Really? Someone enlightened and open to the world around them." Nanna replied with a curious smile.

"Yeah, but then it changed. There was a black spot, it grew and then vanished. I couldn't find anything about it in the book."

Nanna glanced down at the little red book, taking her time to answer.

"Because it is not possible." She finally said, her voice calm and quiet. "Two such opposing auras can't co-exist. You must have imagined it; or you allowed the person he was sitting with to bleed into his aura."

"No, I'm positive-"

"Oh, so you're an expert now? After your first success?" Nanna snapped. "Sorry Mark, you still have a lot to learn."

An awkward silence descended on the kitchen. Nanna looked up at her books above the door and suddenly smiled.

"How about we do something a bit… more?" She got up and pulled down a tatty, leather-bound volume, and carefully opened it. "You can do your first real spell."

Nanna flicked through the pages, before finally settling on one. The old woman sighed, "Oh, this was one of the first spells I mastered."

Nanna set the heavy volume on the kitchen table.

"'To sense a loved one's peril'?" Mark leant in to read the title.

"Yes, I used to use this one when your grandfather worked in the coal mine. I was always paranoid that something would happen, especially when I was pregnant with your Dad." Nanna smiled at the memory of her pregnant-hormone-overreactions. "The spell connects you to a person for about twenty-four hours. It's nothing invasive, you don't get to read their minds or anything; you simply get a warning when they are in trouble."

"We already have that, Nanna. It's called a mobile phone." Mark answered, ducking as a tea towel got lobbed at his head.

"Well it worked for me. I knew the moment your grandad got knocked off his bike, cycling home. I knew where he was, and that I had to get to him. He was in the hospital for a week, bless him, and that leg took months to heal."

"OK, OK, so I need…" Mark leant in to read the instructions. "Eye of newt and toe of frog…"

"That has never been funny." Nanna replied drily. "If you take up witchcraft, you'll have a lifetime of the same jokes and bloody stereotypes."

Mark smiled and read for real. "I need fennel, thistle, and a protection stone."

Nanna pointed to the dried bundles hanging from the ceiling beams. "Help yourself."

Mark looked up at the dried herbs and plants, when he was a young lad, he'd help his Nanna doing regular cooking. He'd been fascinated by how she recognised the different plants, and he'd done his best to learn them. It also helped that his Nanna kept them alphabetically, so she could check her stock at a glance. He carefully removed a couple of sprigs and put them on the table.

Nanna brought out a bag and a small hessian pouch. She opened the bag and spread out the contents.

Mark eyed the collection of stones and crystals. "Which one is a protection stone?"

"You could use tourmaline, but that's more for warding. As we want to focus on sending signals, we'll use haematite, which is that one." Nanna pointed to a particular stone.

"Haematite." Mark repeated the weird word.

"Good, now, in a moment you are going to put the herbs and the stone in the hessian pouch. Two important things – first, while you do this, you must concentrate on the person you want to connect with. Secondly, every small action you make matters. The spell wouldn't work half as well if I gave you the ingredients; when you're manipulating magic, your intention is very important."

Mark frowned, not sure he really understood. "So do I have to say anything?"

Nanna shook her head. "Chanting is simply a way to train your thoughts in the right direction. It's not necessary until more advanced spells. So, who is going to be your guinea pig – Harry?"

"Yeah, that's what I was thinking. Will he notice?" Mark asked.

"If you do it correctly, no, he shouldn't. The connection should only travel one way."

Mark closed his eyes and focussed on his best friend. It wasn't hard to bring him up in his mind's eye, he knew Harry better than anyone else. Trying not to let his concentration waver, he opened his eyes and followed Nanna's instructions. He plucked the dry, crisp fennel leaves and thistle head, and pushed them into the small pouch. He picked up the dark-silver stone, which felt warm in his hand, and added it.

"Now what?"

"Hold it and focus on knowing that Harry is safe." Nanna said quietly. "Then keep the pouch in your pocket to keep connected to the link for the next twenty-four hours."

After he had finished, Mark looked up at his Nanna. "That was easy."

"Well I'm not going to start you off on the hard stuff, am I?" Nanna retorted, moving the unused stones back into their bag.

"I dunno, I guess I was expecting fireworks or something. Anything to confirm that I'd just done something magical."

Nanna smiled. "You're connecting with magic – it's something natural. The flashy stuff is usually a result of going against nature."

Mark frowned a little as he took it all in. The pouch was warm and comfortable in his trouser pocket.

"Go on, bugger off home." Nanna said, clearing the tea tray away. "Your parents will be upset if they find out you've been doing spells instead of chores."

Giving one last stroke to Tigger, who snored gently by the Aga again, Mark made to move. "Thanks, Nanna."

**Chapter Five**

That night, Mark's sleep was interrupted. Something niggled at the edge of his consciousness, as faint as static, but wouldn't let him rest peacefully. As his eyes opened again to see the red digits of his alarm clock reading 3am, he groaned. There should only be one 3 o'clock in the day!

The last time he'd felt like this was when he'd drank too many Red Bulls at a party. Mark pulled the duvet over his head and curled up. He thought about what could possibly have happened today to affect his sleep. Or technically, yesterday.

The only thing that stood out from his regular routine was the lesson in witchcraft with Nanna. Had he done it wrong? Was the connection faulty? Or did it pick up on mental distress as well as physical danger? Was Harry experiencing nightmares – or was he struggling to sleep, too?

Mark sighed, he'd have to ask his Nanna when everyone else woke up. He'd check in with Harry, too. In fact, he could probably do that now, if his best friend *was* awake. He blindly felt for his mobile and tapped out a quick message to Harry. There was no immediate reply, and Mark drifted to sleep with his phone in hand.

*****

When Mark next awoke, there was a soft glow behind the curtains. Even though the sun had yet to rise, the snow gave off a brightness of its own.

Making his way downstairs, he found his Dad frying bacon while his Mum set the coffee to brew.

"I got a text from school, it's cancelled today." His Mum said, smiling. "Lucky you!"

Mark helped himself to some orange juice and looked out of the window, there was a couple feet of snow in most places, with a higher drift up against the shed. The snow ploughs would get to work, and tomorrow everything would be back to normal; but today was freedom.

Well, almost freedom. You couldn't really get anywhere, and nowhere was open, which meant being stuck at home.

"You look tired, are you alright?" His Dad asked, sliding some bacon onto his plate.

"Hmm? Oh, I didn't sleep well."

"You're not coming down with something?" His Mum looked concerned. "I can get some of Nanna's special tea."

Mark shook his head. "No, I'm fine."

His phone buzzed and he picked it up to see a text from Harry expressing his own glee at no school. Before Mark could reply, there was a second text, asking why he'd texted at stupid o'clock.

Mark looked up from his half-eaten breakfast, to his parents. "Sorry, I just need to ring Harry." Before they could argue, he jumped up from the table.

"Yeah?" Harry eventually answered his phone.

"Hey, you OK?" Mark asked casually, while he worked out what to say.

"Hmm, good. Gone back to bed."

"Look, random question, but did you sleep alright last night?"

"Like a log," Harry answered, "why?"

"It's a long story. You know I told you about Nanna training me in witchcraft? Well, she taught me a spell last night that's supposed to tell me when my friends are in trouble. There was something happening last night, and I was worried... about you." Mark finished awkwardly.

"Oh. I don't know what to tell you, Mark. Everything's fine." Harry replied. "Maybe you did it wrong?"

"Yeah, maybe." Mark echoed, not convinced. "OK, go back to sleep, I'll see you tomorrow."

Mark hung up and headed back into the kitchen.

"Everything alright with Harry?" His Mum asked.

"Yes." Mark replied shortly, picking up his fork and poking at the cold bacon on his plate.

\*\*\*\*\*

Mark told his parents he had a lot of GSCE revision to do, but spent most of the morning idly surfing the internet. He'd managed to Google some Christmas ideas; and read the reviews for the films coming out at Tealford cinema.

He looked out of his window to see his Mum shovelling snow from the paths; while his Dad cleared the driveway with a small tractor borrowed from Mr Brown, the farmer next door. Mark helped Mr Brown at weekends and in the school holidays. He supposed if he got very bored this afternoon, he could drive the borrowed tractor back and see if Mr Brown needed any help today.

Seeing his parents hard at work, Mark headed downstairs to the kitchen, with an idea of making dinner for them. When he got there, he found Nanna already stoking the fire for the cooker.

"Hi Mark, how are you enjoying your day off?"

Mark shrugged and headed to the fridge. "It's fine, a bit boring. I just came down to fix some dinner."

"Oh, what are we having?"

Mark looked inside the almost-bare fridge and sighed. "I can probably knock together omelettes. Maybe some oven chips."

"Sounds delicious." Nanna replied, putting her feet up. "You look tired."

Mark frowned, he'd been honest with his parents, but not entirely so. At least he could be completely open with Nanna. "I think there's something wrong with the spell we did yesterday. It kept me up all night, niggling away. But I checked with Harry this morning, and he was fine."

Nanna sat there, running over the possible reasons. "Maybe you lost your concentration. It's fine, you can't expect to get it perfect on your first try."

"No, I was totally focussed on Harry. The whole time, I was... I was..." Mark broke off. His attention had expanded from just Harry, to thinking about school. For a moment Damian had crept to the edge of his thoughts. "I might have *momentarily* thought about the new guy."

Nanna chuckled. "It's good to see you behaving like a normal teenager, distracted by a pretty face?"

"Don't you start." Mark warned. "I've seen you flirting with the farrier at every opportunity, it's disturbing."

"I may be old, but I'm still allowed to enjoy my life." Nanna replied proudly. "Besides, I challenge anyone not to get distracted by the farrier. That man has the body of-"

"I'm not hearing this!" Mark shouted, jumping up and making more noise than necessary in the pan cupboard.

Nanna laughed to herself, and picked up one of her daughter-in-law's magazines.

"So what do I do in the meantime? About this faulty spell?" Mark asked as he tipped frozen chips into an oven tray.

"Huh?" Nanna looked up from reading celebrity gossip. "Oh, I wouldn't bother doing anything. It will wear off in a few hours, so it shouldn't bother you much longer."

Mark frowned, that was not the answer he was looking for. He'd been hoping for a quick break from the spell.

*****

As the afternoon wore on, Mark sat watching the sports highlights with his Dad, when his heart leapt. Mark froze, feeling an intense worry grip his chest.

"Mark?" His Dad glanced over, confused by the worried look on his son's face. "Relax, Leeds could still get some points against Derby next week."

"I'm just going to see Nanna." Mark muttered, jumping up from the sofa and leaving, before his Dad had a chance to quiz him.

Mark forewent the coat and jogged from their front door to Nanna's. He let himself in and followed the sound of Radio 2 until he found Nanna. She was sitting in the small living room, her head in her newest trashy novel. She looked up at the unexpected entrance of her grandson.

"Is everything alright, Mark?"

Mark paced across the small room, trying to physically distract himself from the dull ache in his chest. "I wanted to ask about the peril spell. You mentioned that I'd be alerted – how?"

"Well, I… I imagine that it can vary between people." Nanna replied, her warm brown eyes following him. "When your grandad was hurt, I felt as though everything had stopped. There was an overwhelming sense of something wrong, that didn't fade until I acted on it."

"Like a persistent ache in your chest, a weight on your heart?"

"Yes… why?"

Mark stopped pacing and faced Nanna. "I think the spell has worked, I think someone is in trouble."

"Mark, you can't be sure. We don't know on what level the faulty spell worked – this someone might have just stubbed their toe!"

"But-"

"I mean, do you even know who this alert is from? Have you tried calling Harry and this new kid?"

Mark felt his anxiety rise, he began to pace again to try and settle it. He needed to move, to do something. "No, I… I spoke to Harry this morning, I can call him again. I don't have Damian's number – I don't even know his aunt's name."

Nanna took one look at how upset Mark was, and put her book down. "Right, well you're not going out in that heavy snow. We'll talk to your parents, see if they know how to contact the new guy."

Nanna marched out of her house and around to her son and daughter-in-law's front door. Mark hurried to keep up with her.

As they re-entered his parent's house, Mark paused. He didn't want to go in, it was the wrong direction; he needed to move.

"*You did what?*" His father's raised voice sounded above the TV.

## Chapter Six

Mark knew a family argument was brewing and he didn't want to get stuck in the middle of it right now. Mark saw his coat hanging within reach, and before he processed what he was doing, he had his thick coat on and he was walking through the snow. He turned his head east, gazing at the white horizon.

A thought occurred to him, and he looked down the driveway. He didn't have a car licence, and a car wouldn't get very far; but he *could* drive Mr Brown's tractor.

Before he could change his mind, Mark jogged through the deep snow and climbed into the small red tractor. He pulled out the key that Mr Brown had given him a couple of summers ago, and fired it up. It took a few loud chugs to get the engine going, and Mark looked fearfully back at the house, in case his family heard it.

He put the tractor into gear, raised the bucket, and started slowly down to the road. Once there, he turned left. The road had been partially cleared of snow, but there were still no cars on the road – no one travelled unless absolutely necessary.

As the road veered to the right, Mark followed his instincts and took the next open gateway. The little tractor bobbed and rocked across the uneven ground of the snow-covered field. Mark switched the windscreen wiper on as the snow became thicker, half-blinding his route.

His heart pounded with the sheer stupidity of what he was doing, risking his life in a snowstorm just to pacify an urge. But he'd gone this far now, he knew there was no point turning back.

Mark kept the little tractor heading due east, only swerving off course to find gates between fields. Each time he stopped to open the gates, the snow came higher up his leg, sending a wave of panic.

"It's fine, it will be fine, it will be fine." Mark muttered to himself in time with the loud engine.

He drove on, getting closer to a dark smear on the horizon. A small wooded section that Mark couldn't recognise. *Here.*

Whoever had been drawing him on was close. Mark left the tractor engine running, fearing that he wouldn't be able to start it again; then he jumped out of the cab and pushed his way towards the trees.

"Hello!" He shouted, pausing to hear any reply or sign of life.

*Here.*

Mark trudged forwards, even in the relative shelter of the trees, the snow was a foot deep. "Hello!" He yelled again.

Mark thought he saw a dark shadow move, and headed towards one of the larger trees.

*Here.*

Mark's heart started to thud harder in his chest as he saw someone huddled against the base of the tree. Slowly, sleepily, he raised his head.

"Damian? Why are you here?"

Damian shivered, his blue lips struggling to part to form words.

Mark saw the signs – Damian was slipping towards hypothermia. He had to act now. Mark ducked down and grabbed Damian's arm. "Come on, I need to get you up."

Damian blinked, tears of pain springing to his eyes as his stiff joints were straightened. Mark felt a mild relief that he could still feel pain, that was good news. They didn't have time to waste, and Mark used all his strength to heft Damian to his feet. Damian stumbled, using the tree and Mark to try and stay upright.

Knowing that walking wasn't going to be an option, Mark pulled Damian up onto his shoulders in a fireman's lift. As he started the slow progress back to the tractor, he was thankful for all the years of farm work and hard-earned strength. He was still sweating by the time he reached the headlights' yellow light.

Mark put Damian down on his feet, so he could open the door to the cab. With some difficulty, and enough swearing to make his Nanna proud, Mark managed to push Damian up into the cab. He climbed up behind him, realising how tight and cramped this cab was with two grown lads inside.

Feeling like he was going to overheat at any moment, Mark unzipped his heavy coat. "You'll have more use for this."

With more than a bit of awkwardness, Mark helped Damian get out of his frozen coat, replacing it with Mark's much warmer one.

"Right." Mark took a deep breath. Behind the heavy clouds, the sun had already set, and the world was only going to get darker. Mark suddenly felt more nervous about being able to drive home, than the outward adventure. "We can do this."

Mark revved the engine and started to turn the little tractor, he reasoned that if they just kept heading due west they'd eventually get back to somewhere he recognised.

"Hey, Damian, are you still with me?" Mark asked, careful not to take his eyes off the windscreen.

A groan came from behind him.

"What were you doing out here?"

"Not now." Damian said, so quietly he could hardly be heard above the tractor. "I just need to sleep."

"No!" Mark shouted, twisting in his seat so he could hit the curled-up boy. "You've got to stay awake, until we've got you home and checked out."

Damian grumbled something, too slurred for Mark to make out.

"Tell me... tell me something about you, about life." Mark demanded. "What did you do for fun, before you moved up here?"

"Nuthin' much. Played footie." Damian finally answered, trying to cooperate. "I was striker for the local team."

"Really? Were you any good?" Mark asked, leaning closer to the window, trying to make out anything in the blur of black and white, that would tell him they were on the right track.

"Yeah, not bad. I wasn't about to go pro, but I was the top scorer last year."

"Yes!" Mark shouted, then looked back at Damian. "Sorry, I found the first gate."

Once he'd manoeuvred through, Mark stopped the tractor and jumped down from the cab, pulling the gate closed behind him. The snow and bitter wind cut through his jumper, leaving him shivering as he rushed to climb back into the cab.

"So, football." Mark said as he started to drive again. "You should join our school team, they're absolutely dire and could do with someone on the team who knows which direction the goalposts are."

"You don't play?"

"I've got two left feet." Mark shrugged. "I'm not afraid to admit it."

As the tractor forced its way across the snow-laden fields the conversation turned to music and films and anything Mark could think of. Anything except family, and why Damian was out there in the first place.

Eventually lights blinked on the horizon – at first Mark thought he was imagining them, but soon they burnt bright and real. The white turned to red, as the car drove away from them on the road. Mark turned the tractor to the right, never more glad to see a road.

His heart beat faster as he turned into the familiar driveway. The house was aglow with lights, and had never looked better.

Mark cut the engine and opened the cab door as his parents came sprinting out of the house.

"Mark! You stupid, stupid boy!" His father grabbed his shoulders and gave him a fierce shake, followed by an equally fierce hug. "Don't you *ever* do that again."

"I had to." Mark said, turning back to the tractor. "He needs help. Can you help me get him inside?"

His Mum gasped at the sight of the half-conscious lad curled in the back of the tractor cab. "But how?"

"Not now, Mum." Mark argued.

Between Mark and his Dad, they managed to help Damian walk to the house through the deepening snow. The warmth washed over them all, as they moved inside. Once in the living room, Damian was helped onto the sofa, his limbs shaking in an uncontrollable shiver.

"Shivering, that's good." Mark's Mum stated, quickly switching into nurse mode. "Honey, get him some dry clothes and a blanket. I'll get Nanna, if ever there was a time for her miracle teas, it's now."

Mark watched as his parents went opposite ways out of the room. He stoked up the fire, then returned to Damian. He looked over him carefully, the colour had returned to his skin and lips, but there was still a haunted look in his eyes.

"So are you going to tell me why you were out there tonight?" Mark asked, sitting next to him on the sofa.

Damian refused to meet his eye and looked down at the carpet. "Have you ever... thought the world would be better off without you?"

Mark stared at him, wishing he could unhear that. Before Damian could give an explanation, Mark's Dad walked back in, his arms full with some of Mark's spare clothes, and the guest duvet.

Mark followed his Dad into the kitchen, to give Damian some privacy. He'd never seen his Dad wound so tight, the old man looked like he was getting the kettle on, but he couldn't concentrate on the task.

Finally his Dad rounded on him.

"Do you have *any* idea how dangerous that was? You could have died?" His Dad snapped, keeping his voice low. His normally soft brown eyes were dark shards as he looked at his son. "I have never been more terrified in all my life. You are *never* to do anything like this again."

"I'm sor-"

Before Mark could even get the apology out, his Dad grabbed him and pulled him into another hug. "You probably saved that boy's life. I don't know how you did it, but I'm so proud of you."

Mark wrapped his arms around his Dad, feeling his tension ease.

"But you're grounded, for a month." His Dad said, releasing him and giving him a pat on the shoulder.

"I've still got to buy Christmas presents this weekend." Mark argued.

"Well, you can go do that. On the one condition that you get me something much better than that awful scarf from last year."

Feeling somewhat dazed, Mark moved back into the living room, to find Damian curled on the sofa, the duvet tucked tight about him.

"How you feeling?"

Damian looked up at him with a weak smile, "Like I'll never be warm again."

"If there's anything I can do, let me know." Mark replied.

"Well they do say body heat is the fastest way to..." A female voice interrupted.

"Nanna!" Mark and his Mum shouted at the same time.

Nanna looked down at Damian, smiling. "You must be the new guy."

"You must be the witch." Damian returned, humour in his bright blue eyes.

Nanna nodded. "I like this one."

Mark's Mum gave her a warning look, and pushed past her into the room. She held a thermal flask in her hands, which she gave to Damian. "This is Nanna's miracle tea, sip it slowly."

Damian sniffed at the open flask, "What does it do?"

"It basically warms your blood. It's all herbal." Nanna answered.

"And it won't turn me into a toad?" Damian asked, taking a cautious sip.

"No, but I might."

Mark's Mum butted in before Nanna got warmed up to the banter. "Damian, I don't think you need the hospital, but I would recommend seeing a doctor tomorrow. Now, shall I call your aunt and see about getting you home?"

"No!" Damian's outburst caught everyone by surprise. "Sorry, I..."

Mark frowned, the lad's reluctance plus his previous comment was worrying. He felt a need to keep him under this roof to find out why. Mark turned to his Mum. "It might be safer if he stayed, rather than taking the roads tonight."

His Mum looked between them, then sighed. "Fine, I'll call your aunt to let her know that you're safe and staying over. Dad, can you start dinner? We have an extra guest."

Mark watched as his parents both moved towards the kitchen – he had no doubt that they were looking for an excuse for a private conversation.

"Mark, a word." Nanna said, gesturing towards the hall.

"I'll be back in a min." Mark gave an awkward smile towards Damian, before he followed his Nanna out of the room. "What's up?"

"You were right."

"Really? That's great!" Mark said, grinning. "But... what am I right about?"

"The boy's aura, there's something tainting it."

"What does it mean?"

A look of worry crossed Nanna's face, but she quickly hid it. "I don't know, it's not something I've seen before. I'll do some reading and talk to some other witches... In the meantime, I want you to keep an eye on him."

"That shouldn't be a problem."

Nanna softened a little. "It seems you were meant to get that spell wrong. Right, go on, back to your new friend."

## Chapter Seven

That evening, Damian was looking much healthier and he seemed to be recovering swiftly, although his limbs were stiff and very sore.

Mark's Dad made sure there was enough stew and potatoes for two sittings, and more to spare. After dinner, Damian's eyes were already drooping.

"Come on, I'll show you the guest room."

Mark led the way up the narrow stairs and into the guest room. There was a single bed, with fresh sheets. The old drawers and wardrobe were in the room, making it seem a lot smaller than it was.

"The bathroom's down the hall. Is there anything else you need?" Mark asked.

Damian sat down on the small bed, the frame creaking as he did so. "No, I'm good."

"Well, good night."

"Mark..." Damian called out, as he reached the door. "I wanted to thank you, for today. I have no idea how you found me, but I'm under no illusion as to what would have happened if you hadn't."

Mark held onto the door as Damian spoke, did he sound disappointed that he'd been rescued? Mark sighed and closed the door in case his parents came upstairs; then turned back to Damian. "Why were you out there?"

Damian shrugged, crawling under the duvet, as though that would put an end to the conversation.

"Come on, Damian. You owe me an answer, I risked everything going out there today."

Damian propped himself up on an elbow, his blue eyes meeting Mark's. "You'll think I'm over-reacting, or crazy, but I'm cursed."

Mark moved around the bedposts and perched on the foot of the bed, making it creak anew. "I've told you that I'm a witch, and you think you're the crazy one? Why do you think you're cursed?"

"I don't think, I know. In the last few months, I've lost everyone I've been close to."

"That isn't proof-"

"My parents died in a car crash. My best friend was mugged and beaten, and left in a coma. I moved in with my grandma and she died of a heart attack two weeks later. Don't tell me that isn't proof, and don't you dare say that it's coincidence."

Mark stared at Damian, as he saw the perfect façade crack. He saw pain, immense pain. "I'm sorry, I knew about your parents, but I didn't have any idea..."

"This afternoon, my aunt was in the kitchen cooking and the pan caught on fire. She shouted at me to get out. She got it under control, but I couldn't go back in. It was a warning to me, I know it. If I stayed much longer, she would die." Damian took a shaky breath. "I just started walking, and when the snow started, I wanted it to smother me and clear away all the problems."

"You shouldn't say that. Even if there is a curse, as long as you're alive, we can find a solution." Mark replied.

"We." Damian smiled at the word.

Mark scooted closer, making the bed creak again. "So why only the last few months? What has changed?"

Damian thought for a while, then shook his head. "Nothing, I did nothing. I turned sixteen and life suddenly became hell."

Mark sighed, it wasn't much to go on. "We'll do everything we can, I promise."

"I'm finally having some good luck in my life." Damian said quietly. "I must have been meant to meet you."

Mark suddenly became aware of how close they were, in the privacy of the bedroom. Mark nervously licked his dry lips. Was it his imagination, or was Damian leaning closer?

Mark leant in, sliding his hand closer until the tips of his fingers brushed the skin of Damian's arm, he was sure he was on fire.

The bed creaked again, and Mark pulled back. What was he doing? Damian had nearly died today, he wasn't thinking straight, and he was in no fit state for any sort of romantic intentions. He jumped off the bed, suddenly awkward, running a hand through his dark hair. "Sorry. G'night."

Mark hurried out of the room, closing the door behind him.

"Mark?"

Mark jumped at the sound of his Dad's voice behind him and spun round guiltily. "Night, Dad."

"Uh huh." He stood at the top of the stairs, watching until his son was in his own bedroom, with the door firmly shut.

*****

The following morning, Mark went downstairs to find his Mum and Dad already serving out breakfast to Damian, who sat at the small kitchen table.

"You can borrow more of Mark's clothes for today, Damian." Dad said as he dished out some fried eggs.

Mark's Mum was relegated to getting the hot drinks ready again, which Mark was relieved to see. The last thing he wanted was for Damian to experience his Mum's attempt at cooking.

"I've told work I'll be in late," Mark's Mum said, smiling at Damian, "I can take you to the doctors and drop you off home. I don't think you should go to school today."

Mark looked up from his breakfast, "Do I get the day off, too?"

"Not a chance." His Mum replied quickly.

"But-"

"You stole a tractor yesterday; you're going to school, and then straight home."

"I didn't steal it, I just commandeered it for a couple of hours."

Mark saw the warning signs that his parents' patience was running thin, and sat tight-lipped for the rest of breakfast.

Afterwards, he pulled on his generic school uniform, while Damian got some jeans and one of his nice jumpers. It worried Mark that Damian hadn't said two words to him this morning, and whenever he caught his eye, there was a new wariness in his gaze.

Before Mark left to walk for the bus, he cornered Damian in the living room. "Look, what I said last night about helping you – I meant it. And if you meant what you said about being willing to die, I want you to call me anytime you feel like that again."

## Chapter Eight

School seemed to absolutely drag by; Maths and English seemed to matter less than usual, when witchcraft and curses waited for Mark back home. It was hard being around Harry and Sarah, too; as far as they were concerned, life went on as it always had.

Mark didn't tell them anything about yesterday, how could he? If he told them about his adventure with the tractor, he'd have to tell them why he had gone out, which meant sharing at least some of what Damian had told him. But how could he do that, knowing that he was preoccupied with death and curses; it was far too sensitive to share. Plus, the fact that he'd almost kissed Damian, he wanted to lock that uncomfortable fact away, never to be seen again.

This was the first time that Mark had kept anything from Harry. The secrets hovered behind every conversation and action, screaming at Mark to be told. As the day wore on, he grew quieter and more sullen;

afraid that the whole school could see how awkward he was.

Only Harry seemed to notice and shot a worried look his way. Before he could be cornered after school, Mark hurried to his bus and sat checking his phone for the umpteenth time.

*****

It was normal for Mark to go straight up to Nanna's after school, but today he made his way there with a new determination. He was surprised to hear voices when he opened the door into the warm kitchen; and even more surprised to see Damian sitting and chatting with Nanna.

"What-?"

"I've had a handsome gentleman caller today." Nanna stated with a smug smile.

Damian chuckled at the old woman's comment, but he looked anything but happy. Dark circles and pale skin told how tired he was; and there was a sharp and feverish quality to his blue eyes. "I couldn't stand being home alone this afternoon. Besides, you guys are the only ones I trust to take me seriously. I told my aunt about the curse and she brushed it off as anxiety and teenage overreaction."

"Have you found anything out?"

"I've spoken to some other witches, they have records of curses and demonic involvement, which would match the deaths and the tainted aura." Nanna replied, stating the facts as calmly as she'd discuss the weather.

"So what do we do know?" Mark asked, feeling some excitement stirring.

"Well, I was just quizzing this young man over the origin of this curse. It has to stem from somebody he knows, because nobody curses a stranger." Nanna nodded to Damian.

"But I can't think of a single person that would do this to me; or would have the ability." Damian said with a shrug.

"Which is why we're going to scry for an answer."

"Scry?" Mark wasn't sure where he'd heard that word before.

"We will try to see a vision that will help direct us to our next step." Nanna explained, getting up and rummaging through the cupboards.

Mark watched as she brought out a large bowl and filled it with water, setting it on the table between them.

"You remember what I told you?" Nanna asked Damian, her voice serious.

"Yes." He said, holding out his hand.

"Once the spell starts, there's no going back. I can't change what is shown." Nanna warned.

Mark watched, feeling very much on the side lines, as Nanna took Damian's upturned hand. The old woman picked up a sharp knife, holding it over Damian's palm.

"No!" Mark jumped up from his chair.

"Sit down, boy." Nanna snapped. "All I need is a drop of blood. It will create a much stronger link with his past."

"It's OK, Mark." Damian said calmly, although he winced when the knife finally cut him.

Mark watched the bright red blood drop into the bowl, and slowly disappear, its colour diluted by the water. His Nanna fixed her gaze on the bowl and began to chant beneath her breath; Mark tried, and failed, to hear what she was saying.

When he looked again at the bowl, his breath caught. The water was no longer clean and clear, but full of shadows moving eerily across the surface. As his eyes locked onto the bowl, Mark felt the spell reach out and ensnare him, catching him and refusing to let go. The shadows grew, becoming human in shape, and a brick background filling in behind them.

A man in his late twenties staggered down a quiet street, his blood-shot eyes betraying that he had been drinking. He pulled his once-fine coat about him, so only his dark-blond hair could be seen, and made his way towards the park. At nearly midnight, it was empty. People said that it wasn't worth the hassle from nosy cops, or the risk of a mugging; but the truth was there was something that scared them. Few people in this modern age knew that the park existed over ley lines, and even fewer cared. But they didn't know what could be accomplished if one made the necessary effort.

He knew though, he had been driven by an intense need to succeed. He'd wallowed in failure for too long; no matter what he did, nothing worked out. He was fed up with playing fair, now he wanted what the world owed him.

Finding the perfect spot, he knelt down, and shrugged off his coat to bare his arms. Intoning the words he'd memorised, he took out chalk and drew a pentagram over the short grass. With a sharp knife, he gave shallow slice to his arm, without wavering in his chant.

Once he had finished, the man sat back on his heels, staring into the darkness. He'd been warned that he might have to wait – demons came in their own time. Eventually something rose, darker then the night around it. It was insubstantial, but pulsed with power.

"What do you seek?"

"Success in all things. Riches." The man replied, his voice hoarse.

The thing hovered in front of him, it's aura touching the bare arms of the man, reading him. Satisfied, it retreated a little. "There is always a price."

"Anything."

"The life of your first son."

"Done." The man replied without hesitation. He was unmarried and had no plans for children, so it was no price at all.

The demon growled, its deal made, then started to fade.


Mark gasped for breath, he was overwhelmed by the foreign emotions that washed over him. He had expected something visual, not this.

He looked up to see his Nanna, looking as composed as ever; and poor Damian who looked very shell-shocked.

"That..." Damian finally stirred "That was my Dad."

Nanna quietly packed away the tools of the scry, and excused herself.

"How could he do that?" Damian's temper snapped. The wooden chair screeched as he shoved it back.

"Damian..." Mark stood up, trying to bring him back to somewhere calm.

"It's his bloody fault. He sold me and everybody else to satisfy his sodding greed!" Damian shouted.

"We'll still..."

Damian looked wildly for an escape. "I need to get out."

"No, Damian," Mark barred his path, "You can't run away again."

"Watch me." Damian snapped. "You don't know anything."

Mark grabbed his arms as he tried to barge past, and yanked him back. "There's a reason you're here, Damian. You chose to come here to find out the truth. I'm sorry it hurts, but this is it."

Damian glared at him, but some level of reason had returned. He gripped Mark's arm, keeping him near. "Truth... I was expecting an enemy, not my father."

Mark was suddenly aware that this was the second time in two days that they had been this close. He wanted him this close always, which was one hell of a distraction right now. The fire in his blue eyes might be fuelled by anger, but they were entrancing.

"Do you guys need a minute, or can we crack on?" Nanna asked from the doorway, making them both jump.

"Sorry, Nanna. What do we do now?" Mark asked, letting go of Damian before he did something stupid.

"It's obvious that a demon has a claim on Damian; we have to break that claim. It won't be easy, but luckily for you," Nanna looked to Damian, "we have some of the best witches in the county, and they will all be gathering here, tomorrow night. There's no time better than the Winter Solstice, it is when we are at our strongest."

"Winter Solstice?" Damian repeated the unfamiliar phrase.

"It's the shortest day of the year." Mark explained, fully aware of what was going on after years of Nanna's parties. "It traditionally celebrates the birth of the new year, and longer days ahead. It's also important for witches, as the Solstice is when the fabric between the worlds is at its thinnest, and spells take more effect."

"You've actually been paying attention, I was beginning to wonder." Nanna teased.

"So what do we do?" Damian asked. "Will it be dangerous?"

"We wait until tomorrow. I'll call the rest of the coven to warn them of our plans." Nanna sighed. "There could be some danger, I doubt the demon will back down willingly, but we can contain it as long as you stay strong, Damian."

Damian hesitated, completely out of his depth, then nodded. He was determined to get control of his life again.

"Why don't you two go and relax, forget about it for the rest of the evening. I think Elf is about to start on BBC." Nanna shooed them towards the door.

Despite the seriousness of the situation, Mark smiled. It was his favourite Christmas film. "Come on, I'll make popcorn."

"Sure, planning to battle demons always calls for popcorn." Damian replied drily, but grabbed his coat and followed Mark.

*****

Mark chuckled at a scene between Will Ferrell and James Caan, he'd seen the movie countless times, but it still made him laugh. He glanced towards Damian, and was relieved to see that he was being distracted from the horrors in his life with a bit of Christmas nonsense. Sensing Mark's gaze, Damian glanced his way and smiled.

"So... aside from the crazy stuff, are you missing London?" Mark asked. He couldn't imagine being uprooted from all he'd ever known, being forced to go somewhere totally different.

Damian shrugged. "I guess I haven't had chance to really think about it. I miss being able to jump on a bus or the tube, and going anywhere I like. I was never bored, there was always somewhere to go."

"And up here?"

Damian smirked at an onscreen joke, then turned his attention back to Mark. "I dunno, what do you actually do for fun around here?"

"It's definitely not London. Even if you travel into Tealford, there's not much that impresses." Mark said, trying to rack his brains over what they actually did. It was strange that he always felt busy, and rarely bored. "Me and Harry do a bit of Motocross, have you ridden a dirt bike?"

"Er, no." Damian replied, looking slightly in awe.

"Do you ride horses? Nanna keeps a couple down at the local yard – I'm sure we can lend you a cob." Mark offered. "Horseback's one of the best ways to see the countryside."

"Now you're just having a laugh, can you imagine me on a horse?" Damian said, elbowing him.

They lapsed into a comfortable silence, both watching the film. Eventually Damian spoke up again.

"So what's Tealford High School really like? I felt like everyone was putting on their best manners."

Mark shrugged, he hadn't been to any other schools, nor had there been any new students to share their opinions, so he could only guess. "It's just a school. Same issues as everywhere else, I suppose."

Damian glanced at Mark, a little more nervously. "And, you know... did you get bullied much?"

Mark thought about it for a moment, it was something he hadn't considered for a long time. "Bullied over the witch stuff? Not really, it's a small community and everybody has grown up knowing that my family are witches."

"No, I meant were you bullied for being gay?"

"That obvious, is it?" Mark asked, not sure how he felt about that, he didn't want his sexuality to define him.

"No, one of the chattier girls mentioned it when she was giving me a rundown of the whole school." Damian said, grimacing slightly at the mere memory of the experience.

"Ah." That made Mark feel better, sort of. "To be honest, nobody is that bothered. There was this one guy, a couple of years ago; he tried to make my life hell. Anyway, once my Nanna found out, he had nightmares for a month until he finally apologised and backed off. Maybe everyone's too scared of her."

"I can believe that."

"What was it like at your old school?" Mark asked.

"Bullies are everywhere." Damian said dismissively. "They saw that I was different, which they immediately see as a weakness. I found whenever I played football, I forgot about it for a while and was happy. The more I played, the better I got. Eventually, I got good enough that they started to back off. There were enough important people on my side, that didn't want their striker upsetting..."

Damian's voice tailed off, and he stared vaguely towards the television screen, lost in his own memories.

## Chapter Nine

Mark normally enjoyed the Winter Solstice, primarily because it was a good party, but also because he occasionally got an extra day off school. This morning was truly the start of the Christmas holidays, and it was easy to relax and ignore the impending trial.

Damian had reluctantly gone home last night. Mark would have voted for him to stay again, but his parents had used emotional blackmail and insisted Damian had to make amends with his aunt. A handy, informal note from Mark's Mum, saying that in her nurse's opinion it wouldn't hurt Damian to have one more day to recover, meant that Damian was back about midday.

"Excellent, you can give me a hand building the fire." Mark nodded towards the waste wood that was collected in the garage for this exact purpose every year.

"There's actually a fire?" Damian asked as he struggled to pull a twisted branch free.

"Yeah, we light it as the sun drops to the horizon. It has some traditional link to it, but mainly it just keeps us warm. The party is too big to hold indoors." Mark explained as he carried some broken planks up to the site for the fire. The ground was flat, and he and his Dad had already cleared the worst of the snow. There was a small pile that Mark had already started.

"So there'll be a lot of people here? Your Nanna told me her coven only has a dozen members."

Mark shrugged, "It may be a witch gathering, but it's definitely family-friendly. They bring their partners, kids, grandkids. Mr Brown, the farmer next-door, his family comes every year, too."

By mid-afternoon, everything was ready and Mark's Dad brought round bacon butties to tide them over. It wasn't long after, that people started to arrive, parking on the long drive and walking up.

There was noise and laughter; children were playing games and getting shouted at when they ran too close to the fire. But as the party spirit grew, Damian seemed to shrink back. At one point, Mark noticed that he had vanished completely, and went to find him.

Damian was holed up in the garage, sitting on the work bench, choosing the cold over the crowd.

"Hey, you OK?" Mark asked, his silhouette appearing in the wide garage door.

"I'm kinda freaking out about tonight." Damian confessed. "A few months ago, I didn't believe in witchcraft and demons. I feel so out of control over my own life."

"I understand-"

"How?  How can you possibly understand?  You were brought up with all this!"

Mark sighed, "This whole demon thing is new to me, too.  Can you at least believe that I'm here for you?"

Damian fell silent.  "Sorry, I didn't mean to sound like a prick."

"You've got a good reason."  Mark said, perching next to him.

"Lately, you're the one that's always there; you're the one that makes me feel normal."  Damian said quietly.

Mark turned to see Damian looking his way.  Their faces were mere inches apart in the dark garage, Damian's expression lost to the shadows.  Mark wished that Damian was feeling even half the physical attraction that he was.  He wished that-

Damian leant in and kissed him.

Mark's heart pounded, his hand raised to curl around his collar, pulling him further into the kiss.

"There you guys are!"

Mark pulled away, he'd never been less happy to hear Harry's voice.

"Harry, you absolute bugger!"  Sarah hissed at her boyfriend, before turning to the two guys in the garage.  "Sorry, we were looking for you everywhere.  Nanna said you had something to tell us?"

Mark reluctantly let go of Damian.  "It's your call if we tell them."

Damian licked his lips, before bringing his thoughts into line.  "You trust them, and Nanna approves of them knowing..."

Damian took a deep breath, and proceeded to tell Harry and Sarah everything.

*****

It was nearing midnight, and the party had wound down, only the witches and Mark's family remained. Harry and Sarah also stayed, refusing to leave their friends in peril.

"You can't involve them, they're schoolkids." Mark's Dad argued with Nanna, as preparations were being made.

"This is to save Damian's life, his soul and his bleedin' sanity." Nanna snapped, "Mark chose to take up witchcraft, you should be proud that he's trying to help his friends."

"But Harry and Sarah-"

"Are old enough to make their own choice."

Mark's Mum stepped up and put her hand on her husband's arm. "Darling, you haven't won an argument in your life, don't try now."

Mark cringed at his family giving a public performance, and hurried his friends towards the fire. The witches were already taking their places, and Mark could feel the build of power, he didn't think it would be this strong. It felt like they could do anything, and they hadn't even started yet.

He left Harry and Sarah a few metres away, so they wouldn't interfere with the connection; then he joined the other witches. *The other witches* – those words, and the fact the magic that stirred welcomed him like a brother in the fold, made him shiver with excitement.

Why had he ever doubted that this was the right path for him?

Thirteen of them circled the fire, which had gotten lower, darker and hotter as it burnt through the evening. Mark could see Damian across the circle, standing in front of Nanna, a look of determination in his handsome face. Mark offered him a silent smile, before his attention was suddenly stolen.

The spell had begun. Nanna laid a base spell for protection, before moving to invoke the demon. Across the circle, Mark felt connected to her; her intentions were his intentions. The same feeling pulsed from the other witches around the fire, until it all became rather heady.

The witches were chanting in unison, and on some level Mark felt a panic that he didn't know the words, but as he took a calming breath he realised that he was intoning with the rest. Mark forced himself to relax, and allowed the power of the spell to wash through him.

"Through the mists of time and space;

"Through locks and walls, to this set place.

"We call upon the ancient power;

"Greeted at the midnight hour.

"Link our hopes and hearts as one;

"Til our intentions be done."

Across the way, Nanna was the only one who spoke separately. She looked to the fire, her arms wide. In one hand, she held a bloody knife – Mark's gaze flicked to Damon, and he could see a makeshift bandage on his hand.

"By blood this was done;

"By blood this is undone.

"I call upon the ancient powers;

"To banish evil and release what is ours."

As the old woman repeated the words, the flames from the bonfire froze then became inverted. The fire shuddered and strained, like a living thing. What Mark assumed was a log, broke free and thudded upright into the ground, still burning; but it flexed and drove its claws into the mud. A huge claw and limb, blackened, but burning; Mark's gaze traced it back to its origin, and saw something half-human and half-beast in the fire. It faded between real and solid; and mere sparks in the fire.

Mark pushed down the fear that threatened to rise, and focussed on his chant.

"I order you to relinquish your hold on this boy." Nanna shouted at the demon form.

"You have no power over me, witch. A deal was struck." The voice was guttural and much more terrifying than it had been in the brief scrying vision.

"Not with him, his father. No man can sell his son."

The demon growled, lowering its blazing torso towards Nanna and Damian, who staggered back from the heat. "The father tried to rescind, he had to be removed."

"Then release the boy, you've had your fill of death."

"Deaths do not interest me, I want life." The demon moved, every joint giving a sickening crack, as it turned to face Damian. "His life."

Damian quailed as the thing turned its full attention on him, and he looked to Nanna for help.

"Stay strong." Nanna warned him, before turning to the demon. "You have no claim here."

"You have no power over me, witch." The demon repeated, with a choking, rasping sound of insulting laughter.

"I am the Grand High Witch, I have every power." Nanna yelled.

In the circle, Mark felt another wave of power surge through the connection, it was suffocating and relentless. He glanced at his Nanna, hardly believing that this was all her. The other witches in the circle wavered, then focussed anew at their own chants, sweating at the effort.

Sensing an opponent that it could not overcome, the demon turned to a weaker link. It leered at Damian with black, consuming eyes. "He is already mine. I can make him great. Or I can destroy... again... I have seen his dreams and desires..."

Within the fire, the demon turned again, rearing up and snapping its joints until it faced someone else. Its soulless eyes settled on Mark, the blackness ensnaring him, and numbing him from the connection with the other witches. For a moment Mark felt truly alone against this beast.

"No!" The yell came, and suddenly two gloved hands held onto Mark's.

He took a deep breath and felt the comforting warmth of Harry and Sarah pressed defensively against him. He was no longer alone, and in that moment the demon's hold over him waned.

The demon must have felt it too, and pulled itself up to its full, terrifying height. The flames crackled and roared to life once more. "Three victims instead of one..."

"Enough!" Damian screamed, bringing the focus back onto himself. "You will not hurt anyone. The only victim will be me."

"Damian, stop!" Nanna cried, trying to pull him back.

But it was too late, as Damian thrust his bloody hand in offering to the demon, it crashed down, sending sparks and ash billowing out.

There was a scream, and Damian ran away from the fire, seeking the dark loneliness beyond.

Nanna came stomping over to Mark and his friends, looking incredibly pissed off. "Why he had to act the bloody hero, I don't know, but the whole thing's ruined. You three find him and bring him to my kitchen, while I apologise to everyone."

## Chapter Ten

After grabbing a torch, Mark, Harry and Sarah followed the deep footprints in the snow, all the way to the edge of Mr Brown's farm. Once there, they found Damian huddled against the stone wall, his head in his hands. The poor guy looked ready to tear himself apart, and his head snapped up as they approached.

"I couldn't let it hurt you. I couldn't, no one else is going to get hurt." Damian rambled. "But he's here, I can feel him, in my head, in my heart."

"OK Damian, I know, we're safe because of you." Mark said gently, trying to placate him. "We need to get to Nanna's house, and we'll solve this somehow."

Damian looked up at him with pleading eyes. "We can't let him in; we can't let him near."

Ignoring his babbling, Mark pulled Damian to his feet and helped him back towards the house, Harry and Sarah trailing behind. By the time they returned, the fire was no more than a steaming mess, snow thrown over the last of the embers. The place was empty of people and the cars on the driveway had gone; now that they were no longer needed, everyone had gone home.

The warm and normally familiar kitchen seemed very alien after the ritual outside. The four friends sat very quietly around the kitchen table; they're young faces shell-shocked. Mark's eyes were fixed on Damian. He still looked like Damian, despite the clenched fists and flush to his skin as his heart worked overtime.

They all jumped when Nanna stomped into her kitchen, still looking rather peeved.

"We almost had him." She muttered. "All he needed was a willing vessel, and you just had to go and give him one."

"Nanna, leave him be." Mark snapped, knowing that Damian had been through enough.

"What happens now?" Sarah asked meekly, holding Harry's arm out of nervous habit.

"Now... now we all go to bed."

Mark stared at Nanna, waiting for the real answer, as surely she wasn't serious.

Nanna sighed and sat down at the table, directly across from Damian. "Look at me."

Damian reluctantly lifted his eyes to meet Nanna's, the normally light blue much darker now.

"You're in there, aren't you?" Nanna muttered, then sat back, satisfied. "There's nothing to be done at this time. The demon's hold on Damian is in its infancy, and as such it's as tangible as a shadow. It might show hints of itself, but we need it to be somewhat more solid before we can expel it, which might take months."

"He's got to live with a demon inside of him?" Harry asked, looking rather disgusted.

Nanna nodded, "I'm afraid so."

"Is that dangerous?"

"To be honest, Harry, I don't know. As long as we can keep the demon at bay for the next few months, in theory it should pose no threat." Nanna replied, less than convincing. "But I think it's safest if Damian is always with Mark or me, we can keep the demon at bay."

Mark jolted up, shocked at the idea of keeping that beast from this night under control. That seemed bloody impossible, whether the demon possession was in its infancy, or not. "I can do what now?"

"I'll teach you what you need to know." Nanna said, with a gentle smile to her grandson. "I might have forgotten to mention that you come from a *strong* witch bloodline."

"Yeah, Grand High Witch?" Mark replied, raising a questioning brow.

Nanna tutted. "It's just a title, boy. You'll only be accessing the power of your ancestors when I think you're ready."

The old woman looked at the four teenagers sitting around her kitchen table, they all looked so worn out already, yet she knew that they had a hard time ahead of them. She wished that it wasn't that way, and she knew that she would do everything in her power to make it easier.

"Right you lot, it's nearly two in the mornin'. Bed." Nanna stood up, making her chair screech as she pushed it back. "You can crash in the living room, I'll bring some blankets down."

The adrenaline that had pushed them all on had finally crashed and they were not going to argue. The teenagers stood up, and shuffled into the living room. Sarah, being the only one short enough, got dibs on the tiny sofa, and the boys made themselves comfortable on the floor.

Mark stayed wide awake. Despite the fact that he was physically exhausted, he was still wired from tonight. Even the mere memory of the power and magic the coven had amassed made his heart race with the thrill of it.

Next to him, Mark could hear the steady breathing of Harry and Sarah, both fast asleep. When he turned to Damian, he could see his open eyes, somewhat dazed, but still awake. Mark could see where his private thoughts were leading him, and he didn't like it.

"Damian..."

"Stop. Don't try and make everything OK." Damian interrupted, keeping his voice low so as not to disturb the sleepers. "I've ruined everything."

"All you did was make a choice." Mark argued, quietly. "Maybe it wasn't the best choice, but it was very bravely done."

"And now I have to live with the consequences. I have this this inside of me, infecting me." Damian muttered. "You have to understand, the only thing I can do now is leave. I can't let it hurt any of you."

Mark sighed, imagining they were going to have this argument a lot. "You heard Nanna, we're your best hope of controlling this thing. Which means I have every excuse to be with you."

Damian closed his eyes for one long, lingering moment. When he opened them again he was caught between what he wanted and what was responsible.

Mark hesitantly reached out and in the almost-darkness, he traced the curve of Damian's cheek, his fingertips pausing at his soft lips. "It looks like you're stuck with me..."

**Merry Christmas**

Christmas Day normally felt unexciting after the Winter Solstice.  Mark still loved it, the presents and being allowed wine with dinner; but after the big annual party on the 21st December, Christmas was very quiet in comparison.  Nanna would come around, of course; and Mark's Dad was in charge of the cooking, although they all had their own little jobs (Mark was always in charge of the mash and roasties); and his Mum was in charge of the copious drinks, and equally copious embarrassing photos.

This year was rather different, and Mark couldn't help but think that they were on to a new tradition!

His Mum managed to persuade Damian and his aunt to join them for Christmas Dinner, which was perfect. Mark had been worrying how Damian's mood would dip, being alone with his aunt; surely lots of noise and people would help to distract.

Mark met Damian's aunt for the first time. She was younger than he had been expecting, only thirty years old. He found her to be very pleasant, and suddenly felt guilty that he'd been so consumed with everything Damian, he hadn't given the aunt another thought. She'd lost her sister and her brother-in-law; she was suddenly raising a sixteen-year old who appeared to be a trouble-causer... Nanna tried to persuade Damian to tell her the truth, but he refused to. Mark had a feeling that Damian was scared that his last remaining family member would reject him if they knew he was possessed.

Later that afternoon, once their own family requirements had been appeased, Harry's parents brought him and Sarah round. The old house was so full of warmth and life! Squeezing past each other, careful not to spill the mulled wine; handing round the biscuit tin. Mark grinned at the thought that it almost felt like they were in one of those cheesy Christmas adverts.

As the evening wore on, Damian sat on the small sofa next to Nanna. Mark sat on the thick rug, using Damian's legs as a backrest. His Dad had just brought round a tray of turkey and cranberry sandwiches, which were so delicious that everyone tried to find room for them. Harry had brought his guitar and was perched on the arm of the big chair, playing Christmas carols. Mark listened, realising how long it had been since he last heard him play; he was much better than Mark remembered. Harry's Mum and Sarah were squished into the seat of the big chair, giggling and singing along to the carols.  Mark wished he could say that they sounded just as good but, yeah, flat notes all round.

They might have had a hard time recently, and there was definitely danger ahead, but Mark couldn't help feeling that just for a moment, for a day, this was perfect. They had a full week and a half before school ensnared them once more.  Mark had wondered how Damian's demon possession might affect the average school day, but that had only given him a headache.  They would simply face each day and each problem as it came, together.

Smiling to himself, he got up and took his empty plate to the kitchen.  Once he'd finished loading the dishwasher, two strong hands caught about his waist, and he could feel warm breath on the back of his neck.

"I have been trying to get a moment alone with you for hours." Damian stated.

Mark turned in his hold to face him. "Really?  What on earth for?"

Damian smiled, leaning in closer before pausing.  His now-dark blue eyes flicked upwards and he chuckled. "What do you know, mistletoe..."

Other books by K.S. Marsden:

## **Witch-Hunter**

The Shadow Rises (Witch-Hunter #1)

The Shadow Reigns (Witch-Hunter #2)

The Shadow Falls (With-Hunter #3)

Kristen: Witch-Hunter (#2.5) ~ *avail only through website*

James: Witch-Hunter (#0.5) ~ *coming soon*

Sophie: Witch-Hunter (#0.5) ~ *coming soon*

## **Enchena**

The Lost Soul: Book 1 of Enchena

The Oracle: Book 2 of Enchena ~ *coming soon*

74975324R00050

Made in the USA
Columbia, SC
13 August 2017